August 16, 2023

ISBN: 978-1-939484-59-8

https://martamoranbishop.com

Cover by Stephen Walker

https://srwalkerdesigns.com

A special thank you to Robert W Walker, Stephen Walker, and Tricia T La Rochelle

THE MICE OF BARNVILLE

EPISODE TWO

FORGING THE HOMESTEAD

BY

MARTA MORAN BISHOP

QUESTIONS AND ANSWERS

"Oh no, oh Gawd help us! Something is coming out of the doorway. It isn't coming to get us, is it? What could it be? I hope it hasn't hurt anyone or killed Uncle Horace or Uncle Redd," wailed Chester, cowering and peering from behind Amos.

"Why don't we just wait and see, Chester?" Amos calmly replied. Impatiently pushing his way closer to the front.

Chester limped closely behind Amos, shaking all over. "Look, it's Uncle Redd. Perhaps we'll learn something."

Through the chorus of voices shouting, "Uncle Redd, what's in there?" Ryker's voice yelled the loudest.

"Will it be our new home?" Amos shouted.

"Is there anything horrible in there? Is Uncle Horace okay?" Chester yelled.

"Silence!" yelled Tucker, holding the crowd back. "Move back, don't crowd him."

Uncle Redd, scratching his nose with his tail, squinted from the sunlight as he stepped into the daylight amidst the shouting of the small cluster of his nephews, cousins, and son.

"If you quiet down, I'll tell you."

You could barely hear the mice breathing. It had become so quiet it sounded as if some of them were holding their breath. The tall and small, the squat and thin, whiskers all a-twitter, they stood silently.

"As to the first question, € doesn't appear to be anyone living in there at this time, and it looks as if no one has been for a long time. But our warrior mice are still checking, to be sure."

"Can we go in yet, Uncle Redd?" Joshua anxiously asked.

"Not yet, Joshua," he said to the youngster," but we have a job for you and your cousin Bertram, and it's an important one."

"What do you want us to do, Uncle Redd?"

"Take your cousin and go around the side of this building through the jungle over there and find out what is on the other side. We need to know if it's safe to open up a door on the south side, and if we do, will it be an easier way to move Aunt Tabby and the little ones in?"

"Okay, Uncle Redd. Come on, Bertram. Let's get going. I want to see the inside, but exploring is almost as much fun."

"Ahh, Joshua, I'm hot. Why do I have to go?"

"Stop being so lazy, cousin. Think of it as another adventure."

"Alright,-alright. Joshua, I'm coming." Bertram exclaimed, as he pushed his way through the crowd, nearly knocking a few of his relatives off the cliff in the process.

The two started toward the side of the building, scampering as fast as they might. “Hurry up, Bertram,” Joshua called over his shoulder.

“I’m doing the best I can, Joshua.”

“I know you are Bertram, but we need to make better time. Everyone is depending on us.”

They stopped as Uncle Redd called. “Oh, and if there is anyone up there, we need to know their schedule, too. Are the horses and humans out there? Do they leave the area, or do they stay nearby?”

“Alright, Uncle Redd,” Joshua shouted back as the two cousins disappeared into the jungle beside the barn, which they all hoped would become their new home.

SEEKING

After the group sitting on the small ledge between the barn and the rocks watched Joshua and Bertram round the corner of the building, until they were lost from view in the jungle of high grass and reeds. Then they all turned back to Uncle Redd.

"Now where was I?"

"Is it a good place for our home, Uncle Redd?"

"To answer Amos' question. We can build an entire city under this barn. We'll call it Barnville. That is, if it's safe on the southern side, and we can move the little ones, Aunt Tabby, and the elderly, up here."

"Are you sure it's safe in there? There aren't any mousetraps, snakes, weasels, rats, or other predators?" Chester cried.

"It is. The warriors just need a bit more time to make sure. Now I need a few more of our builders to come up here to help Uther and Farren finish the worm and beetle farms. Tucker, please keep everyone else out for now."

Ryker and Amos started scampering toward Uncle Redd.

"Move over, please," Ryker stated as politely as he was capable of being considering the unruly mouse that he was.

"Amos, who's here to protect me if you go in? You are so big and strong. I need you," Chester shrieked.

Knowing he couldn't ignore the question, Amos answered hurriedly. "Stay with Gus, Chester. He'll guard you, won't you, Gus?"

The paunchy warrior shrugged, chest swelled, and he replied, "Sure, cousin. I'll take care to protect Chester."

"Thank you, Gus," Chester uttered, limping toward his second cousin. "What does Uncle Redd need them for?"

"It appears we will have indoor farms full of worms and beetles. Chester, isn't that wonderful? I just wish it was me going in with him, too."

"It will be wonderful if we don't have to go out all the time to scavenge for food. But if you went inside, what would happen to me?" Chester asked, his fur quivering and whiskers twitching."

"You'd be fine, Chester. We all know you had your foot crushed in that mousetrap and it has made you lame. It must have been very painful. I hope it doesn't hurt much now. We will help keep you safe. We know you are vulnerable because you can't move as fast. But please grow a little backbone."

"Don't say things like that, Gus." He cringed as if he'd been slapped while pleading with his second cousin.

"I'm sorry, Chester." Gus answered with a sigh, watching his cousins talking to Uncle Redd. "Shush now, I'm trying to hear what Uncle Redd is saying."

Standing close to Gus, still fearful, but feeling too ashamed to admit it, Chester stood silently, trembling.

“I can’t hear a word. What’s happening?” The small crowd left on the ledge murmured as they tried to move closer to the doorway.

“Move back, don’t crowd anyone. We don’t want anyone to get hurt. You’ll all get your turn to go into Barnville soon,” Tucker yelled at the group. “Abe, please help me keep them all calm.”

Most of the warriors held their spears crossed over their chests. Not exactly threateningly, but it could appear so to those still waiting to get inside Barnville. Abe, holding his spear in the air, said. “No problem, Tucker.”

“Put your spear down, Abe, across your chest is enough. You don’t need to look as if you will throw it at one of our relatives.”

“Oh Gawd.” Chester squeaked as he watched Uncle Redd, Amos, and Ryker disappear through the doorway under the barn.

“Tucker, what are they going to do in there? Did you hear?”

“Did anyone bring any food? I’m hungry.” Basil yelled.

“All I know is that Amos and Ryker are going to help the builders. As far as food goes. I’d suggest you forage a bit. I don’t believe anyone brought something to eat with them. There must be flatter land in front of the barn. Those horses down there wouldn't be climbing up these cliffs and through the jungle to get into their rooms." Tucker finished.

I wonder how Joshua and Bertram are making out, Gus," Chester said plaintively. "Do you think they will make it back safely?"

"I'm sure they will, Chester. Joshua is a master of adventure and good at finding all sorts of things."

ANSWERS

"Hold up, Joshua. You're moving too fast for me. There are big ruts and holes, and a lot of rocks here," pudgy Bertram yelled ahead to his cousin, while plucking a bug off one of the tall fronds of overgrowth. All this scurrying about is making me hungry," he said, stuffing the bug into his mouth.

"We're almost to the front, Bertram. Stop thinking about your stomach for a change. We are on a mission for Uncle Redd and Uncle Horace."

"I'll try, Joshua, but it doesn't seem to stop it from growling," he called ahead to his slender cousin. *Just because you are so thin doesn't mean we all are,* he thought as he hurried, without success, to catch up.

As they reached the front of the wooden building, Joshua peered around the corner. No one is in the front right now, Bertram. Let's look around."

"Do you think it is safe, Joshua?"

"I do, but if we are to move Aunt Tabby, and the little ones up here, we must hurry. The horses will come back up from the backfield, and I suspect the farmers will come soon to feed them."
"Farmers are so mean to us, Joshua. Do you think they will come soon?"

"Not for a bit anyway, and the horses just went back down into the backfield, so it's obviously not dinnertime yet. So we can do a quick look around and go back and report what we have found. Okay, Bertram. You take the stalls. I'm going to look to see if the land is this flat beyond the fencing."

As the two young mice split up, each going in a different direction, both kept a keen lookout for predators. Joshua called to his paunchy cousin, "I'll meet you back here, Bertram!"

"OKY-DOKY," Bertram answered, his snout twitching, trying to catch the scent of anything edible.

Creeping into the first stall, Bertram sniffed the smell of something sweet that hung in the air. Hunting around, he found it, and stuffed his tiny mouth with a few pieces of grain, just before putting the rest into a pouch he carried at his waist. He filled it up almost to the brim before he exited the stall to meet his cousin.

With eyes squinting from the bright sunlight, he exited into the field, almost bumping into his lanky cousin.

"Woah, Bertram," Joshua said, startled, sidestepping out of his cousin's way.

"Sorry, Joshua, I didn't mean to bowl you over. Look at what I found on the floor in the stall." He stated, opened his pouch to show his cousin the grain. "Here, have a bit. It is absolutely delicious."

Taking a single piece of grain, Joshua savored it before getting down to business. "It looks as if you've found a substantial food source for us, Bertram. Good job. Is it safe in there for us to go in and out?"

"It appears it will be whenever the humans or horses aren't in there. I didn't see any snakes, cats, rats, or other horrid creatures. What did you find out?"

"The land past this field looks pretty flat, as far as I can tell. Though this sandy field won't provide any cover when we bring the rest of our family up here."

"Do you think it will be a serious problem?" Bertram asked.

"No, not even for the little ones. If everyone hurries, they can manage to come this way."

"That's good!"

"Did you look to see if there was a door on this side?"

"I didn't, but we can look for one now," Bertram excitedly replied.

"Over here cousin. I believe this was a doorway once upon a long time ago. Here, help me shove this rock out of the way."

"Do you suppose the farmers filled it in with sand and put this rock on top?"

"Probably, Bertram."

After a great deal of effort, the two young mice rolled the huge rock a bit, but just enough so it no longer covered what appeared to be what might have been a doorway, once upon a time.

Bertram wiped the sweat from his brow with the back of his paw and sank down to the ground. “I’m about done in, Joshua.” He gingerly took more grain from his pouch.

“I know what you mean. All this scurrying around and rolling rocks is hard work. But we can’t sit here. Everyone is depending on us.”

“I suppose you are right,” the pudgy little mouse said as he pushed himself back up on his paws. “I’m about as ready as I will ever be, Joshua.”

“Let’s be off then,” was the only answer he received before he followed his cousin around the corner of the building. Through the tall fronds, over the rocks, and through the ruts to the back side of the building, they hurried.

BACK SAFELY

As the group of mice sat between the cliff and the barn, awaiting news, Bertram and Joshua appeared.

“There they are!” screamed Chester. “They don’t look hurt either.”

“Stay back. You all don’t want to push them off the cliff. Let them come through! Abe, please hold everyone back a bit. I’m going to poke my head inside the barn to call Uncle Redd.”

“Yo.” answered the heavyset, but muscular mouse.

“What you got there, Bertram?” Dag asked, after Tucker had gone a bit into the doorway. “What did you bring, Joshua?”

“I brought sweet food. I found it in the horse’s rooms in front. Joshua brought water.”

“Hand the bag over, Bertram.”

“Don’t bully my cousin, Dag. I don’t care that you are a warrior and bigger than me. It will be up to Uncle Horace and Uncle Redd to dole out the bits. As it will be with the water I brought back?” The lanky little mouse stood up for his cousin, getting right in Dag’s face.

Just as Dag was about to get rougher on his young cousins, Tucker came through the doorway, followed by both Uncle Horace and Uncle Redd.

"What's going on out here?" Uncle Horace asked, squinting through the spectacles that hung off the end of his long nose. The sunlight made it difficult to see, but the old mouse sensed the tension in the air.

"Bertram found some food, and it smells delicious," stated Basil and Dag. "And Joshua brought water."

"We will make sure everyone gets a share of the food and water. Now, before anyone else comes in, we want to have a conference with Joshua and Bertram. Please come with me, you two," Uncle Horace said as he turned and started back through the doorway.

"We're coming, Uncle Horace," Joshua and Bertram said in unison, happy to be away from Basil and Dag.

"Why can't we all come in now, Uncle Horace?" yelped a chorus of voices.

"The rest of you can come in soon. As far as when, we need all of you to do a few things before you come in. Tucker will give you instructions." Uncle Redd added sternly. "Tucker, please have Basil and Dag find a few of those dead bamboo pieces, and the rest of you each gather at least two or three of those large leaves each to use as plates. When you've gathered those things, we'll send someone out for you." He said as he followed the group back through the doorway.

Once inside the new town, Uncle Horace stated kindly to the two adventurers. "Come with me, you two," Joshua, what happened to the string I gave you?" Looking at

Joshua's pants, the corners of his mouth pulled down into a frown. "Come along now."

"I used it to tie up the water pouch, Uncle Horace."

"Well, I suppose that was a good idea at the time. Bertram, please give your pouch to Uther or Farren. They are in charge of the food."

"Yes, sir," Bertram replied.
Holding his pants up, Joshua followed Bertram and Uncle Horace into the town. Uncle Redd brought up the rear, for he had stopped to say a few last words to Tucker. Without pomp, Joshua handed Farren the pouch filled with grain.

"Gasper, come over here, please," Uncle Redd called to the short little engineer. "This should fascinate you."

Gasper turned around and rapidly made his way toward the worm and beetle farms. "Joshua, it looks like you've made something to carry water. I'd like to study it if you don't mind?" Gasper said politely, always interested in new inventions.

"Sure, Gasper." Joshua proudly stood, somehow taller, again hiking his pants back up again.

"Why, this is fascinating, Joshua," began Gasper. "Perhaps you should become one of our apprentices in the engineering trade." Gasper closely studied the water pouch. 'I think I can use this design and improve on it a bit."

Hearing this, Joshua gasped and replied, "Really?"

"Leaves are great but do break down easily," he said, pondering the leaf pouch as he carried it over and poured the liquid into a small hollowed out rock, and handed Joshua back his string.

"I'll think about it, Gasper," Joshua replied. *I'm not sure I'm ready to start studying and stop being an adventurer just yet,* he thought as he tied the string back around his pants.

"What is everyone doing, Uncle Horace?" Bertram asked as he looked around at his cousins scurrying around, all hard at work on different projects.

"Well, Gasper's group is digging to make separate areas for each family. Usher and Farren have been busy building a farm to keep the beetles and worms in."

"Raul and his warriors have finished checking every nook and cranny and are now helping both Gasper's group with the building and Usher and Farren to expand the farms. They are getting things ready in Barnville to bring Aunt Tabby, Aunt Maisie, and the rest of our families into our new home," added Uncle Redd, who was now standing next to his older brother, Horace, "Should we send Lamorat and Raul out to bring some of the plates those who are still outside picked? They can come in afterwards. But those who have been working inside will get their food first."

"Good idea, brother. It'd be a waste of time to have Joshua and Bertram repeat everything."

Strutting out the door of Barnville, Lamorat and Raul were met by a crowd of their cousins and brothers yelling, "Can we go in yet?"

"Yes, but first give us a bunch of those plates. We'll take them in. Those who have been working inside will get their food first. As you go in, don't crowd anyone, don't be pushy, and get in line behind the workers. Uncles Redd and Horace want all of you to get your food and take your places around the outside of the circle. But make sure those who are taller sit in the back and the shorter fellows up front."

"Why do we have to sit on the outside?" complained Basil.

"That is all I know. Anything else you'll find out inside," Tucker said, peering at each of his fellow mice through his thick spectacles.

"What will they do with the bamboo bits?" Chester grumbled nervously?"

"You'll all see soon. Tucker, would you help to make sure everyone comes into Barnville in an orderly fashion, after giving us the bamboo pieces and plates, of course?"

"Sure, Raul. Now listen up, you all, pass some of the plates you collected up here, so Raul and Lamorat can bring them into Barnville."

"Will we hear what Joshua and Bertram have to say, won't we?" Basil spoke in a demanding voice.

“Of course, it’s all of our business,” Tucker replied, frowning at his slightly tubby fellow warrior.

RESPITE & PLANS

Uncle Redd spotted Lamorat and Raul the minute they entered the town carrying a stack of leaves, and called. "Gasper, you and your builders please each grab a plate from the stack that Raul and Lamorat brought in, and get your food and sit down near the front. You all will need to finish your food early and get back to work as soon as we know what the layout is. If we can open the front door, you'll need to get started on that immediately," Uncle Redd added, eyeing his brother for approval.

"Coming Uncle Redd." The short, pudgy little mouse signaled his fellow builders. After picking up a plate, they all rushed over to the farms. "It is so cool that we will have indoor gardens." Gasper stated, while Usher and Farren filled the plates with beetles and worms. As each mouse had his plate filled, he went to sit down. Each of them was delighted to sit in the front to hear the news.

Uncle Horace continued. "Hey, everyone, get a plate of food and come over here. Most of you will stay on to help finish the beginnings of our new town."

Redd agreed, adding, "As soon as you've got your food, please sit down." The small group of mice happily agreed to a break and chatted among themselves as they ate and waited for the others to come in.

"As soon as everyone else is in here, we can hear what our two adventurers have to say," assured Redd.

Once everyone has eaten and heard what Joshua and Bertram have to say, Uncle Redd and I will give you directions on what we need to concentrate on next."

"As you say, Uncle Horace." Abe said with a sheepish look.

"Raul, please have the others come in now."

Strutting out of the doorway, Raul called. "You all can come in now. But mind your manners, as Uncle Horace and Uncle Redd told you."

"Is it safe in there, Raul?" Chester called from behind Amos.

"It is Chester. Come on, everyone, don't push each other, come on in, and leave the extra plates on the stack near the gardens. They'll be needed by the rest of our family when they get here."

As the big and the tall, the squat and the skinny, the small, and the stout, moved toward the doorway, each of them pulled a couple more leaves off the brush that lined the road as they scampered to the doorway and into their new home.

After spending so long out in the sunlight, it took a few minutes for each of them to regain their natural ability to see in the darkened room. They looked about in awe. The vast space was already taking on the appearance of a small town. The area was lit with little flames coming from the small hollowed out rocks the engineers had designed.

"It's so huge," Abe said, looking around at the enormous chamber.

"It's massive. I wonder what the builders are doing?" Amos asked his cousin.

"It looks to me like they are moving dirt to divide into individual areas for each family to live in."

"Wow, wouldn't that be cool? I don't ever recall every family having their own home. This will be a city," Chester butted in. "What do you suppose they are doing over there?"

"Everyone, take your plates over to the gardens that Uther and Farren have set up."

"How about I serve the worms, and you dole out the bugs, Uther?" Farren softly asked his short, balding cousin.

"Sounds like a plan, Farren," Uther replied to his husky, hairy cousin, as he filled the large leaf that Bertram was holding with beetles. "I must admit, though, that they are hard to keep in everyone's leaf plates."

"The worms aren't much easier, Uther." Farren replied, pushing the worms back into the folds of the leaf for the next mouse in line.

"What about the sweets that Bertram brought?" Basil demanded.

With their plates full of food, they sat down on the outside of the circle, the smaller ones in the front, the larger mice in the back. Every mouse ate its lunch.
In a stern voice, Uncle Horace yelled from his seat. "In answer to Basil's questions. Eat your main course first. You all need the protein. The grain will be given out soon."

"Sweets are wonderful and yes, they contain many nutrients, too. Today, we will, as Horace says, eat them in order," Uncle Redd stated, frowning at each young mouse.

"ALL RIGHT!" The mice shouted in agreement, tiny mouths full, their sharp teeth biting into the succulent beetles and slurping down the long worms.

THE NEWS

"Can Joshua please get on with it? We want to hear about what's up front," Yelled Dag, grouchily. Still unhappy that he'd been unable to get hold of the bag of grain from Bertram earlier.

Directing a frown toward Dag, Uncle Horace spoke. "Now that everyone is here and has their food. Let's hear the news that you two have for us." Pushing his spectacles back up, he added, "Now, which one of you wants to begin?"

"I will if you don't mind, Bertram?"

"Go ahead, Joshua." Bertram retorted, his mouth full of beetles. "I'm hungry. I'll fill in my part as you go."

"Bertram and I made our way through the jungle on the side of the barn," Joshua started, a worm hanging out of his mouth as he talked.

"We know that part, Joshua. Let's move to what you found out in front, please," Uncle Redd impatiently said, drawing a bit of a frown from his older brother.

"Well, I saw a huge flat field with a wooden fence around it."

"And then?" Uncle Horace pulled on his eyebrows and pushed his spectacles back up his nose once again.

"Well, past the fence, the land is pretty flat, though there are the usual brush and weeds on the other side. It doesn't appear we'd have any problems bringing Aunt Tabby, Aunt Maisie, or the little ones through it. Though they'd all need to hurry, there is no grass or anything else for cover. It's just sand as far as the eye can see until one gets beyond the fence. I think it'd be clear sailing to get them into Barnville once the door is opened."

"Though if they don't hurry across the sandy field, someone might see them, or a predator might catch them." Added Bertram.

"There is that to consider. I believe we'll need to send a few extra warriors." Redd uttered, looking at his brother.

"I agree, Redd."

"Do believe we have any time constraints, Joshua?"

"Well, the horses, come up to the front field for shelter from the sun and to take a nap. Then there is their feeding time, when the humans come to feed them and clean out their stalls."

"Does it appear there is a schedule for all this traffic?" Uncle Redd butted in.

"Yes, but they just went down back, and I think we have a few hours before the humans return, and after they eat, they go down back for another few hours."

"Do the humans stay up there for a long time?" asked Uncle Horace.

"I think only sometimes, Uncle Horace."

"Joshua and I really struggled to move the gigantic rock away from the old front door. It exhausted me. I didn't think I'd make it back here. But the grain bits helped to give me strength."

"Where did you get the grain, Bertram?"

"Joshua had me check out the horse's rooms. It was in there on the floor. I guess the horses don't eat it all and leave some behind."

"You two did a great job. Now finish your meal," Uncle Horace called out.

"You can all get back to work now." Uncle Redd stated.

Uncle Horace raised his small fingers to single to the builders and engineers. Clearing his throat and gazing at the group with his rheumy old eyes, Uncle Horace added, "Gasper, please have your crew open that door in the south. And pick out some of your builders to carve out the bamboo to make sleighs."

"Will do Uncle Horace." The formouse motioned for his crew to follow him.

"Farren, Uther, please finish collecting the beetles and worms and put them into the farms you've built. Pick a few mice to help you."

"Abe and Amos, will you help us?" Uther asked politely.

"Okay," they said in unison, happy to have a project to keep them busy.
"What kind of time limit do we have?" Abe politely asked, ever the kindest of mice.

"There is a lot of coming and going from the back to the front of our new home, so the door needs to be opened quickly by Gasper and his engineers. Those that have been busy making sleighs for you all to take down to pick up the rest of our family will need to help work on the doorway." Uncle Horace stated calmly as he smoothed his gray eyebrows.

"I think Basil and Dag can help carve the bamboo, don't you, Horace?" Uncle Redd added. "After all, we have a time limit before the horses and humans come back up to the front, so we will need to get a move on."

"Sounds like a plan, Redd," Horace said with a grin.

"What about the rest of us, Uncle Horace?" Chester asked.

"We have jobs for each of you. While you finish your lunch, we will assign each of you some tasks."

TASKS

"What's next, Uncle Horace?" Dag hastily asked.

"Those who have been working inside have had little to no break, and neither have Joshua and Bertram. After all, they have been rushing around while the rest of you have been sitting outside in the open air." Tucker said impatiently to Dag. "You and your brother will do your part now and later, too."

Merle said quietly, "Tucker is right. Settle down. We still have much to do today, and I am hoping we can move Aunt Tabby, Aunt Maisie, and the little ones in today. If we all get ourselves in a frenzy, arguing among ourselves, that won't happen."

Everyone sat quietly, waiting anxiously for their uncles to speak.

"Thank you, Uncle," the pudgy Bertram replied. "Though I'm tired, and though I know we will need to keep working, I'd like to rest a bit before I start again. I feel like I could sleep for a week."

"What will we do with the sleighs?" Gus asked.

"The little pups, the infirm, and those who are with pups and can't move quickly will need to be pulled. We must get everyone into our new home before the horses come up for supper," Uncle Redd replied."

"I think Basil and Dag can help carve the bamboo, don't you, Horace?" Uncle Redd added. "After all, we have a time limit before the horses and humans come back up to the front, so we will need to get a move on."

"Sounds like a plan, Redd," Horace said with a grin.

"Great idea, brother, and we don't have a lot of time to do it in. Basil and Dag and their cousins are a perfect choice," cut in Uncle Horace.

"How much time do we have, Uncle Horace?" Sebastian inquired.

"As soon as the sleighs are done, you must leave to get the others. Gasper will have the door open by then. Chester, I want you to go with this group."

"I don't walk very fast, Uncle Horace."

"No, but you are good with the children and those who are injured. So, you will have to hurry as fast as you can. I'm sure your cousins will help you."

"Can I add to that, brother?"

"Go ahead, Redd."

"Basil and Dag, you will go with the rest of the warriors, and you will listen to Tucker. You are not to bully anyone, even if they are moving slower than you'd like."

Hanging their heads, ashamed of being singled out by their uncle, they said. "Yes, sir."

"Bertram, we'd like you to make your way out the front door to see if you can find some shavings, or hay to make nests for Aunt Tabby and the pups."

"Okay, Uncle Redd. What about Joshua?"

"We have another task for Joshua."

"Redd looked at Horace for a minute and turned back to Joshua. "We'd like you to climb up and see what is above the wood ceiling, and if there's anything that might make our lives better down here."

"I can do that, Uncle Redd. Is there anything in particular you'd like me to look for?"

"You're a bright boy. We believe you'll know it if you see it, but in particular if you can find anything, we can use to make a nest for your Aunt Tabby and all the pups." Uncle Horace added, staring at the young mouse.

"I'm on it, Uncle." The young mouse scampered away toward the mound of dirt at the edge of the wood ceiling.

"Now, those that will pull the sleighs grab one of them and line up for final instructions, please."

"Okay, Uncle Horace." was all that the group said. Most of the mice were determined to do their part. Basil and Dag had been put in their place and were ready to prove themselves to their uncles, as well as the rest of the community.

"When you get the rest of our family to the fence line. Please send someone out to check and see if there is time to move everyone across the enormous field of sand before the horses come up to the front for supper."

"If we get there too late, and the humans and horses have returned, what then, Uncle Redd?" asked Abe.

"Wait in the brush till the horses go to the backfield and the humans have left. Then the women, children, the infirm, should be brought across first. It must be the priority of all the warriors to protect them."

"We can do that, Uncle Redd," answered Abe.

"Now scuttle as fast as you can. We want to move everyone in before dark," added Uncle Horace.

"I hope they make it all right."

"Redd, with Raul, Merle and Tucker in charge, they'll make it," Horace said to his brother as they watched their sons and cousins cross the field.

Chester limped along with Abe at his elbow, just in case he needed a hand. Merle pulled on his whiskers, his eyes looking around for any predators that might lurk in area. Meanwhile, Dag and Basil followed behind, spears at the ready, trying to get everyone to move more quickly without appearing to bully anyone.

Back under the barn came a loud squeak. "Uncle Redd, Uncle Horace!" Joshua called, scrambling down from the wall of sand that reached to the ceiling.

"What did you find, Joshua?"
"There is a room up there, but I don't think it's one we want to spend a lot of time in. It's full of mouse poison. But I pulled this off some of the blankets I found in the room. Will it help?" Joshua pulled out a pile of string wrapped in a pouch made of double layers of wool.

"That is a terrific find, Joshua. And if your cousin brings back anything from the horses' rooms, we will have enough to make nests for all the pups and for Aunt Tabby, too."

"If I may add, Horace, Joshua's find is remarkable. Gasper, can you pull together a few of your brothers and make up some nests?"

Gasper hurried over, took one look at what Joshua had brought, and replied, "Absolutely, we'll get started right away."

"Gasper, do you think there is enough to make a nest for Maisie?" he said in a sad tone.
"Judah, I'm sure Gasper has plenty of thread to make a nest for Maisie. If not, Joshua will need to go get a bit more. It might help her, if she has a place to call her own."

"Thank you, Uncle Horace," Judah replied with the first small smile they'd seen in a long time from him. Just before Gasper rushed off to round up some of his cousins for the project, Bertram came rushing to the door as fast as his squat body would carry him.

RESCUE

"Help!" Bertram yelled, pulling a large leaf full of grain through the doorway. "A huge cat is chasing Chester and the little ones. Raul, Dag, Basil, and I think it's Cousin Festus are holding it off. But I think they need help, and the rest of the warriors are pulling sleighs."

"Coming Bertram," yelled Judah and Joshua's father, Theodore, a tall, handsome mouse. As he went to carry the shavings, leaves, and stiff hay their nephew had earlier piled high before the last stall, through the doorway.

"Coming Merle," Sebastian yelled back.

"Get every able-bodied mouse out there now. Help Merle, pull the sleighs with the little ones and Aunt Tabby into Barnville!" Uncle Horace shrieked.

Nearly every mouse not needed for other projects streamed out the doorway, running as fast as they could to lend a hand to Merle and Tucker. Dag, Basil, and Raul were using their long spears to fend off the tiger stripped cat, while Festus twirled a large spike in his gigantic hands.

Gasper rushed over. "Can I be of help?"

"Yes, Gasper!" Redd's face, red with terror for those outside. "That'd be wonderful if you and your crew could quickly make a few nests. Aunt Tabby is on her way and due to pup anytime now. We can finish the rest after all the little ones are inside. Everyone else has gone to help pull the sleighs, so it will be up to you and your crew."

"I'll get right on it," Gasper replied.

As the rest of the mice helped pull the sleighs, Tucker, and Gus, joined Basil, Dag, Raul, and Festus, who were fighting off the deadly cat. Spears up and swinging, the warriors protected the flank as Dag yelled. "Chester, get in one of the sleighs with the little ones."

Just in the nick of time, the caravan of mice made it through the doorway, pulling the sleighs behind them.

"Bring Aunt Tabby over here," called Gasper. "I have a nest waiting for her."

"Thank you, Gasper," Jethro frantically said, as he helped his mate into the nest. "She's beginning to pup."
Pointing with his cane, Uncle Horace said firmly. "Chester, bring the little ones to that quiet corner over there. The rest of you help Gasper get some more nests made for them. Chester, please calm the little ones down while we make their nests."

"Come on with me young'uns," Chester said patiently, hiding his own panic as he limped along with the young'uns. His soothing tone calmed them, and they followed him into the quiet corner. Still afraid, but knowing that Chester would tell them a story, and somehow it would help, they sat in a circle around him. Their gigantic eyes looked fearfully around the room. But they sat quietly and listened to Chester, for he was a master storyteller.

"Usher, Farran, please bring the little ones something to eat," Uncle Redd called out.

"Yes, sir." They replied, piling up plates full of food for the little ones.

Aunt Maisie scanned the room, terror in her eyes as she clung to her mate Judah, who pleaded, "Gasper, do you have a place ready for my Maisie yet?"

"Bring her over here, next to Aunt Tabby, Judah. Perhaps it will calm her down."

"I fear she's in shock."

"Judah, when things are calmer and everyone is in our new home, I believe she'll come out of it. Stella, please come over here and help comfort Maisie." Uncle Horace said.

The stout, fair mouse made her way over, put her arm around Maisie, and began crooning to her. "She'll be okay, Uncle Horace. She just needs a bit of time, and quiet."

"Let us pray our warriors can hold off that cat until everyone is inside," Uncle Horace stated, just as the last of their family slid through the doorway into their new home. With the warriors following closely behind them. Raul, Dag, Basil and Cousin Festus stayed just inside the doorway, holding off the cat who sat just outside the doorway with their spears.

"Is everyone safe?"

"I think so, Uncle Redd." Tucker looked around the cavern before answering his father.

"Festus, I'm glad you made it back in time to help." Raul said to his cousin, who was covered in dirt from ears to toes.

"Me too, cousin. Though it could have been a little less hairy of a situation. Still, a good fight is always fun," Festus answered as he took another poke at the cat's paw with a spear, as it continued to reach into the mouses doorway, under the barn.

"I suspect the cat will leave as soon as the horses or humans arrive. Do you think you can hold it off till then?" Uncle Redd asked.

"It can't get in the town, so we don't need anyone here now," replied Raul.

"I'll stay for a bit. Seeing that huge paw in the doorway may frighten the young'uns, and I'd like to make sure that it remembers what happens when it pokes its paw down here." Festus uttered with an enormous grin.

Thank you for reading The Mice of Barnville—Episode Two—Forging The Homestead.

I hope you enjoyed episode two of The Mice of Barnville, and will look forward to Episode three.

If you enjoyed The Mice of Barnville, as with all authors, I hope you will take the time to leave a review. Reviews help us become better writers and learn what our readers liked and didn't like.

www.ingramcontent.com/pod-product-compliance
Lightning Source LLC
LaVergne TN
LVHW040213110826
845155LV00030B/714

* 9 7 8 1 9 3 9 4 8 4 5 9 8 *